A BOOK OF ELEPHANTS

Compiled by Katie Wales
Illustrated by David McKee

PARENTS' MAGAZINE PRESS
NEW YORK

Contents

First published in the United States of America 1977 by Parents' Magazine Press
Illustrations, typography and general arrangement Copyright © 1977 Kaye & Ward Ltd
Printed in Great Britain

Library of Congress Cataloging in Publication Data
Main entry under title:
A Book of elephants.
1. Elephants–Legends and stories. (1. Elephants– Fiction. 2. Short stories) I. Wales, Katie. II. McKee, David.
PZ5.B64   (E)   76-23139
ISBN 0-8193-0891-9
ISBN 0-8193-0892-7 lib. bdg.

The publishers are grateful to the following for permission to use copyright material in the English edition of this book:
Chatto and Windus for *The Elephant's Picnic* by Richard Hughes from DON'T BLAME ME AND OTHER STORIES; A. P. Watt and Son, Executors of the Estate of Mrs George Bambridge, Macmillan Co. of London and Basingstoke and Doubleday & Co. Inc., New York, for *The Elephant's Child* from THE JUST SO STORIES by Rudyard Kipling, copyright 1900 by Rudyard Kipling; William Heinemann Ltd, London and Macmillan Publishing Co. Inc., New York, for *The Elephant*, from PILLICOCK HILL by Herbert Asquith; Little Brown and Co., Boston, for *Eletelephony* from TIRRA LIRRA: Rhymes Old and New by Laura E. Richards, copyright 1932, 1935 Laura E. Richards; The Bodley Head, London, for *How Rabbit Fooled the Elephant and the Whale* from TO READ AND TO TELL edited by Norah Montgomery and for *The Stamping Elephant* from THE ANITA HEWETT ANIMAL STORY BOOK; Dennis Dobson for an abridgement of ELMER: THE STORY OF A PATCHWORK ELEPHANT by David McKee; Oxford University Press for *The Elephant is a Pretty Bird* from THE LORE AND LANGUAGE OF SCHOOLCHILDREN By Iona and Peter Opie; Hamish Hamilton Children's Books Ltd for two short extracts from DRAGONS, UNICORNS AND OTHER MAGICAL BEASTS by Robin Palmer, copyright © Robin Palmer, published in the USA by Henry Z. Walck Inc., a division of David McKay Company Inc. and reprinted by permission of the publishers. Librarie Hachette, Methuen Children's Books, London, and Random House, New York, for *The Story of Babar* by Jean de Brunhoff translated by Merle Hass, copyright 1933 renewed by Random House for the USA, reprinted by permission of the publisher; Walt Disney Productions for *The Story of Dumbo;* and to Mr A. F. Scott for his help in tracing the poem *The Blind Men and the Elephant* by John Saxe.

The Elephant's Picnic

Elephants are generally clever animals, but there was once an elephant who was very silly; and his great friend was a kangaroo. Now, kangaroos are not often clever animals, and this one certainly was not, so she and the elephant got on very well together.

One day they thought they would like to go off for a picnic by themselves. But they did not know anything about picnics, and had not the faintest idea of what to do to get ready.

"What do you do on a picnic?" the elephant asked a child he knew.

"Oh, we collect wood and make a fire, and then we boil the kettle," said the child.

"What do you boil the kettle for?" said the elephant in surprise.

"Why, for tea, of course," said the child in a snapping sort of way; so the elephant did not like to ask any more questions. But he went and told the kangaroo, and they collected together all the things they thought they would need.

When they got to the place where they were going to have their picnic, the kangaroo said that she would collect the wood because she had a pouch to carry it back in. A kangaroo's pouch, of course, is very small; so the kangaroo carefully chose the smallest twigs she could find, and only about five or six of those. In fact, it took a lot of hopping to find any sticks small enough to go in her pouch at all; and it was a long time before she came back. But silly though the elephant was, he soon saw those sticks would not be enough for a fire.

"Now *I* will go off and get some wood," he said.

His ideas of getting wood were very different. Instead of taking little twigs he pushed down whole trees with his forehead, and staggered back to the picnic-place with them rolled up in his trunk. Then the kangaroo struck a match, and they lit a bonfire made of whole trees. The blaze, of course, was enormous, and the fire was so hot that for a long time they could not get near it; and it was not until it began to die down a bit that they were able to get near enough to cook anything.

"Now, let's boil the kettle," said the elephant. Amongst the things he had brought was a brightly shining copper kettle and a very large black iron saucepan. The elephant filled the saucepan with water.

"What are you doing that for?" said the kangaroo.

"To boil the kettle in, you silly," said the elephant. So he popped the kettle in the saucepan of water, and put the saucepan on the fire; for he thought, the old juggins, that you boil a kettle in the same way you boil an egg, or boil a cabbage! And the kangaroo, of course, did not know any better.

So they boiled and boiled the kettle, and every now and then they prodded it with a stick.

"It doesn't seem to be getting tender," said the elephant sadly, "and I'm sure we can't eat it for tea until it does."

So then away he went and got more wood for the fire; and still the saucepan boiled and boiled, and still the kettle remained as hard as ever. It was getting late now, almost dark.

"I am afraid it won't be ready for tea," said the kangaroo. "I am afraid we shall have to spend the night here. I wish we had got something with us to sleep in."

"Haven't you?" said the elephant. "You mean to say you

didn't pack before you came away?"

"No," said the kangaroo. "What should I have packed anyway?"

"Why, your trunk, of course," said the elephant. "That is what people pack."

"But I haven't got a trunk," said the kangaroo.

"Well, I have," said the elephant, "and I've packed it! Kindly pass the pepper; I want to unpack!"

So then the kangaroo passed the elephant the pepper, and the elephant took a good sniff. Then he gave a most tremendous sneeze, and everything he had packed in his trunk shot out of it — tooth-brush, spare socks, gym shoes, a comb, a bag of bull's-eyes, his pyjamas, and his Sunday suit. So then the elephant put on his pyjamas and lay down to sleep; but the kangaroo had no pyjamas, and so, of course, she could not possibly sleep.

"All right," she said to the elephant; "you sleep and I will sit up and keep the fire going."

So all night the kangaroo kept the fire blazing brightly and the kettle boiling merrily in the saucepan. When the next morning came the elephant woke up.

"Now," he said, "let's have our breakfast."

So they took the kettle out of the saucepan; and what do you think? *It was boiled as tender as tender could be!* So they cut it fairly in half and shared it between them, and ate it for breakfast; and both agreed they had never had so good a breakfast in their lives.

Richard Hughes

The Elephant's Child

In the High and Far-Off Times the Elephant, O Best Beloved, had no trunk. He had only a blackish, bulgy nose, as big as a boot, that he could wriggle about from side to side; but he couldn't pick up things with it. But there was one Elephant — a new Elephant — an Elephant's Child — who was full of 'satiable curtiosity, and that means he asked ever so many questions. *And* he lived in Africa, and he filled all Africa with his 'satiable curtiosities. He asked his tall aunt, the Ostrich, why her tail-feathers grew just so, and his tall aunt the Ostrich spanked him with her hard, hard claw. He asked his tall uncle, the Giraffe, what made his skin spotty, and his tall uncle, the Giraffe, spanked him with his hard, hard hoof. And still he was full of 'satiable curtiosity! He asked his broad aunt, the Hippopotamus, why her eyes were red, and his broad aunt, the Hippopotamus, spanked him with her broad, broad hoof; and he asked his hairy uncle, the Baboon, why melons tasted just so, and his hairy uncle, the Baboon, spanked him with his hairy, hairy paw. And *still* he was full of 'satiable curtiosity! He asked questions about everything that he saw, or heard, or felt, or smelt, or touched, and all his uncles and his aunts spanked him. And still he was full of 'satiable curtiosity!

One fine morning in the middle of the Precession of the Equinoxes this 'satiable Elephant's Child asked a new fine question that he had never asked before. He asked, "What does the Crocodile have for dinner?" Then everybody said, "Hush!" in a loud and dretful tone, and they spanked him immediately and directly, without stopping, for a long time.

By and by, when that was finished, he came upon Kolokolo Bird sitting in the middle of a wait-a-bit thorn-bush, and he said, "My father has spanked me, and my mother has spanked me; all my aunts and uncles have spanked me for my 'satiable curtiosity; and *still* I want to know what the Crocodile has for dinner!"

Then Kolokolo Bird said, with a mournful cry, "Go to the banks of the great grey-green, greasy Limpopo River, all set about with fever-trees, and find out."

That very next morning, when there was nothing left of the Equinoxes, because the Precession had preceded according to precedent, this 'satiable Elephant's Child took a hundred pounds of bananas (the little short red kind), and a hundred pounds of sugar-cane (the long purple kind), and seventeen melons (the greeny-crackly kind), and said to all his dear families, "Good-bye. I am going to the great grey-green, greasy Limpopo River, all set about with fever-trees, to find out what the Crocodile has for dinner." And they all spanked him once more for luck, though he asked them most politely to stop.

Then he went away, a little warm, but not at all astonished, eating melons, and throwing the rind about, because he could not pick it up.

11

He went from Graham's Town to Kimberley, and from Kimberley to Khama's Country, and from Khama's Country he went east by north, eating melons all the time, till at last he came to the banks of the great grey-green, greasy Limpopo River, all set about with fever-trees, precisely as Kolokolo Bird had said.

Now you must know and understand, O Best Beloved, that till that very week, and day, and hour, and minute, this 'satiable Elephant's Child had never seen a Crocodile, and did not know what one was like. It was all his 'satiable curtiosity. The first thing that he found was a Bi-Coloured-Python-Rock-Snake curled round a rock.

"'Scuse me," said the Elephant's Child most politely, "but have you seen such a thing as a Crocodile in these promiscuous parts?"

"*Have* I seen a Crocodile?" said the Bi-Coloured-Python-Rock-Snake, in a voice of dretful scorn. "What will you ask me next?"

"'Scuse me," said the Elephant's Child, "but could you kindly tell me what he has for dinner?"

Then the Bi-Coloured-Python-Rock-Snake uncoiled himself very quickly from the rock, and spanked the Elephant's Child with his scalesome, flailsome tail.

"That is odd," said the Elephant's Child, "because my father and my mother, and my uncle and my aunt, not to mention my other aunt, the Hippopotamus, and my other uncle, the Baboon, have all spanked me for my 'satiable curtiosity — and I suppose this is the same thing."

So he said good-bye very politely to the Bi-Coloured-Python-Rock-Snake, and helped to coil him up on the rock again, and went on, a little warm, but not at all astonished, eating melons, and throwing the rind about, because he could not pick it up, till he trod on what he thought was a log of wood at the very edge of the great grey-green, greasy Limpopo River, all set about with fever-trees.

But it was really the Crocodile, O Best Beloved, and the Crocodile winked one eye — like this!

"'Scuse me," said the Elephant's Child most politely, "but do you happen to have seen a Crocodile in these promiscuous parts?"

Then the Crocodile winked the other eye, and lifted half his tail out of the mud; and the Elephant's Child stepped back most politely, because he did not wish to be spanked again.

"Come hither, Little One," said the Crocodile. "Why do you ask such things?"

"'Scuse me," said the Elephant's Child most politely, "but my father has spanked me, my mother has spanked me, not to mention my tall aunt, the Ostrich, and my tall uncle, the Giraffe, who can kick ever so hard, as well as my broad aunt, the Hippopotamus, and my hairy uncle, the Baboon, *and* including the Bi-Coloured-Python-Rock-Snake, with the scalesome, flailsome tail, just up the bank, who spanks harder than any of them; and *so*, if it's quite all the same to you, I don't want to be spanked any more."

"Come hither, Little One," said the Crocodile, "for I am the Crocodile," and he wept crocodile-tears to show it was quite true.

Then the Elephant's Child grew all breathless, and panted, and kneeled down on the bank and said, "You are the very person I have been looking for all these long days. Will you please tell me what you have for dinner?"

"Come hither, Little One," said the Crocodile, "and I'll whisper."

Then the Elephant's Child put his head down close to the Crocodile's musky, tusky mouth, and the Crocodile caught him by his little nose, which up to that very week, day, hour, and minute, had been no bigger than a boot, though much more useful.

"I think," said the Crocodile — and he said it between his teeth, like this — "I think to-day I will begin with Elephant's Child!"

At this, O Best Beloved, the Elephant's Child was much annoyed, and he said, speaking through his nose, like this, "Led go! You are hurtig be!"

Then the Bi-Coloured-Python-Rock-Snake scuffled down from the bank and said, "My young friend, if you do not now, immediately and instantly, pull as hard as ever you can, it is my opinion that your acquaintance in the large-pattern leather ulster" (and by this he meant the Crocodile) "will jerk you into yonder limpid stream before you can say Jack Robinson."

This is the way Bi-Coloured-Python-Rock-Snakes always talk.

Then the Elephant's Child sat back on his little haunches, and pulled, and pulled, and pulled and his nose began to stretch. And the Crocodile floundered into the water, making it all creamy with great sweeps of his tail, and *he* pulled, and pulled, and pulled.

And the Elephant's Child's nose kept on stretching; and the Elephant's Child spread all his little four legs and pulled, and pulled, and pulled, and his nose kept on stretching; and the Crocodile threshed his tail like an oar, and *he* pulled, and pulled, and pulled, and at each pull the Elephant's Child's nose grew longer and longer — and it hurt him hijjus!

Then the Elephant's Child felt his legs slipping, and he said through his nose, which was now nearly five feet long, "This is too butch for be!"

Then the Bi-Coloured-Python-Rock-Snake came down from the bank, and knotted himself in the double-clove-hitch round the Elephant's Child's hind-legs, and said, "Rash and inexperienced traveller, we will now seriously devote ourselves to a little high tension, because if we do not, it is my impression that yonder self-propelling man-of-war with the armour-plated upper deck" (and by this, O Best

Beloved, he meant the Crocodile) "will permanently vitiate your future career."

That is the way all Bi-Coloured-Python-Rock-Snakes always talk.

So he pulled, and the Elephant's Child pulled, and the Crocodile pulled; but the Elephant's Child and the Bi-Coloured-Python-Rock-Snake pulled hardest; and at last the Crocodile let go of the Elephant's Child's nose with a plop that you could hear all up and down the Limpopo.

Then the Elephant's Child sat down most hard and sudden; but first he was careful to say "Thank you" to the Bi-Coloured-Python-Rock-Snake; and next he was kind to his poor pulled nose, and wrapped it all up in cool banana leaves, and hung it in the great grey-green greasy Limpopo to cool.

"What are you doing that for?" said the Bi-Coloured-Python-Rock-Snake.

"'Scuse me," said the Elephant's Child, "but my nose is badly out of shape, and I am waiting for it to shrink."

"Then you will have to wait a long time," said the Bi-Coloured-Python-Rock-Snake. "Some people do not know what is good for them."

The Elephant's Child sat there for three days waiting for his nose to shrink. But it never grew any shorter, and, besides, it made him squint. For, O Best Beloved, you will see and understand that the Crocodile had pulled it out into a really truly trunk same as all Elephants have to-day.

At the end of the third day a fly came and stung him on the shoulder, and before he knew what he was doing he lifted up his trunk and hit that fly dead with the end of it.

"'Vantage number one!" said the Bi-Coloured-Python-Rock-Snake. "You couldn't have done that with a mere-smear nose. Try and eat a little now."

Before he thought what he was doing the Elephant's Child put out his trunk and plucked a large bundle of grass, dusted it clean against his fore-legs, and stuffed it into his own mouth.

"'Vantage number two!" said the Bi-Coloured-Python-Rock-Snake. "You couldn't have done that with a mere-

smear nose. Don't you think the sun is very hot here?"

"It is," said the Elephant's Child, and before he thought what he was doing he schlooped up a schloop of mud from the banks of the great grey-green, greasy Limpopo, and slapped it on his head, where it made a cool schloopy-sloshy mud-cap all trickly behind his ears.

"'Vantage number three!" said the Bi-Coloured-Python-Rock-Snake. "You couldn't have done that with a mere-smear nose. Now how do you feel about being spanked again?"

"'Scuse me," said the Elephant's Child, "but I should not like it at all."

"How would you like to spank somebody?" said the Bi-Coloured-Python-Rock-Snake.

"I should like it very much indeed," said the Elephant's Child.

"Well," said the Bi-Coloured-Python-Rock-Snake, "you will find that new nose of yours very useful to spank people with."

"Thank you," said the Elephant's Child, "I'll remember that; and now I think I'll go home to all my dear families and try."

So the Elephant's Child went home across Africa frisking and whisking his trunk. When he wanted fruit to eat he pulled fruit down from a tree, instead of waiting for it to fall

as he used to do. When he wanted grass he plucked grass up from the ground, instead of going on his knees as he used to do. When the flies bit him he broke off the branch of a tree and used it as a fly-whisk; and he made himself a new, cool, slushy-squshy mud-cap whenever the sun was hot. When he felt lonely walking through Africa he sang to himself down his trunk, and the noise was louder than several brass bands. He went specially out of his way to find a broad Hippopotamus (she was no relation of his), and he spanked her very hard, to make sure that the Bi-Coloured-Python-Rock-Snake had spoken the truth about his new trunk. The rest of the time he picked up the melon rinds that he had dropped on his way to the Limpopo — for he was a Tidy Pachyderm.

One dark evening he came back to all his dear families, and he coiled up his trunk and said, "How do you do?" They were very glad to see him, and immediately said, "Come here and be spanked for your 'satiable curtiosity."

"Pooh," said the Elephant's Child. "I don't think you peoples know anything about spanking; but *I* do, and I'll show you."

Then he uncurled his trunk and knocked two of his dear brothers head over heels.

"O Bananas!" said they, "where did you learn that trick, and what have you done to your nose?"

"I got a new one from the Crocodile on the banks of the great grey-green, greasy Limpopo River," said the Elephant's Child. "I asked him what he had for dinner, and he gave me this to keep."

"It looks very ugly." said his hairy uncle, the Baboon.

"It does," said the Elephant's Child. "But it's very useful," and he picked up his hairy uncle, the Baboon, by one hairy leg, and hove him into a hornets' nest.

Then that bad Elephant's Child spanked all his dear families for a long time, till they were very warm and greatly astonished. He pulled out his tall Ostrich aunt's tail-feathers; and he caught his tall uncle, the Giraffe, by the hind-leg, and dragged him through a thorn-bush; and he shouted at his broad aunt, the Hippopotamus, and blew bubbles into her ear when she was sleeping in the water after meals; but he never let any one touch Kolokolo Bird.

At last things grew so exciting that his dear families went off one by one in a hurry to the banks of the great grey-green, greasy Limpopo River, all set about with fever-trees, to borrow new noses from the Crocodile. When they came back nobody spanked anybody any more; and ever since that day O Best Beloved, all the Elephants you will ever see, besides all those that you won't, have trunks precisely like the trunk of the 'satiable Elephant's Child.

Rudyard Kipling

THE ELEPHANT

When people call this beast to mind,
They marvel more and more
At such a *little* tail behind
SO LARGE a trunk before.   *Hilaire Belloc*

ELETELEPHONY

Once there was an elephant,
Who tried to use the telephant —
No! no! I mean an elephone
Who tried to use the telephone —
(Dear me! I am not certain quite
That even now I've got it right.)

Howe'er it was, he got his trunk
Entangled in the telephunk;
The more he tried to get it free,
The louder buzzed the telephee —
(I fear I'd better drop the song
Of elephop and telephong!)   *Laura Richards*

How Rabbit Fooled the Elephant and the Whale

One day little Brother Rabbit was running along liperty, liperty, when he heard the Whale and the Elephant talking. And this is what they were saying:

"You are the biggest animal on land, Brother Elephant," said the Whale, "and I'm the biggest animal in the sea. If we join forces, we can rule all the other animals in the world, and have our own way about everything."

"Very good, very good," trumpeted the Elephant, "that suits me, Brother Whale, We'll do that."

"You won't rule ME," thought little Brother Rabbit, and away he ran and fetched a very long, very strong rope. He took out his big drum and hid it in the bushes. Then he walked along the shore till he met the Whale.

"Brother Whale, you're the strongest animal in the sea," he said. "Please will you come and help me pull my cow. She's stuck in the mud a mile from here and I can't pull her out."

"I'll help you, little brother," said the Whale, fairly
bursting with pride.

"Then I'll tie the end of this rope to you," said the Rabbit,
"and I'll tie the other end of it to my cow. When all is ready
I'll beat on my drum, then you'll know it is time to pull on
the rope. You'll have to pull very hard, for my cow is very
heavy and she's stuck very deep in the mud."

Huf!'' said the Whale. ''Just leave it to me. I'll have her out in no time!''

So little Brother Rabbit tied the rope to the Whale and off he ran liperty, liperty, till he came to the Elephant.

''Brother Elephant, you are the biggest animal on land,'' he said, ''please will you help me. My cow is stuck in the mud a mile from here and I can't pull her out.''

"I'll help you! I'll pull her out!" trumpeted the Elephant. "No trouble at all!"

"Then I'll tie the end of this rope to you," said the Rabbit, "the other end is already tied to my cow. But first I'll go back and make sure it is secure, and when all is ready I'll beat on my drum. When you hear that, pull! Pull as hard as you can for my cow is very heavy!"

"Just leave it to me," said the Elephant grandly, "I could pull twenty cows!"

"Of course you could," said little Brother Rabbit, "only be sure to pull gently at first, then harder and harder till you get her."

When he had tied the rope tightly round the Elephant's trunk, Brother Rabbit ran off into the bushes. There he beat his drum.

The Whale began to pull, and the Elephant began to pull. They pulled and pulled till the rope tightened and was stretched as hard as could be.

"Goodness," said the Elephant, "this must be a heavy cow!"

"Gracious!" said the Whale. "This cow is stuck mighty fast!" He pulled harder and the Elephant pulled harder.

Soon the Whale found himself sliding towards the land, for the Elephant had managed to turn the rope round his trunk. This made the Whale so cross with the 'cow' that he dived head-first into the water, right down to the bottom of the sea. That WAS a pull.

The Elephant was jerked off his feet, and came slipping and sliding down the beach, into the surf. He was terribly angry.

He braced himself with all his might, and pulled as hard as he could. Up came the Whale out of the water.

"Who's pulling me?" spouted the Whale.

"Who's pulling *me*?" trumpeted the Elephant.

AND THEN THEY SAW EACH OTHER.

"I'll teach you to fool me!" fumed the Whale.

"I'll teach you to play 'cow'!" trumpeted the Elephant.

Then they began to pull again. This time the rope broke. The Whale turned a somersault, and the Elephant fell over backwards.

The Elephant wouldn't speak to the Whale, and the Whale wouldn't speak to the Elephant. So the pact between them was broken.

As for little Brother Rabbit, he sat in the bushes and laughed and laughed and laughed.

American Folk Tale

The Elephant is a pretty bird,
It flits from bough to bough,
It builds its nest in a rhubarb tree,
And whistles like a cow.

Traditional

31

Fabulous Beasts

GANESHA

In India, where the elephant is a beast of great importance, we find Ganesha, who has the head of an elephant on a human body. He is also described as having four arms and four hands. He rides from place to place on the back of a rat, which must be a monster to bear his great weight, for Ganesha is far from thin. He is supposed to be fond of eating sweet cakes.

MAKARA

Just as the mermaid is half fish, half human, the makara is half fish, half animal. For example, he is sometimes described as having the head of an elephant and the body of a fish. Then again he may have the head and even the forefeet of another animal, but also combined with the fish's body and tail. He is generally large and lives in the ocean rather than in lakes and streams.

Robin Palmer

The Stamping Elephant

Elephant stamped about in the jungle, thumping down his great grey feet on the grass and the flowers and the small soft animals.

He squashed the tiny shiny creatures and trod on the tails of the creeping creatures. He beat down the corn seedlings, crushed the lilacs, and stamped on the morning glory flowers.

"We must stop all this stamping," said Goat, Snake, and Mouse.

Goat said, "Yes, we must stop it. But *you* can't do anything, Mouse."

And Snake said, "Of course she can't. Oh no, *you* can't do anything, Mouse."

Mouse said nothing. She sat on the grass and listened while Goat told his plan.

"Scare him, that's what I'll do," said Goat. "Oh good, good, good, I'll scare old Elephant, frighten him out of his wits, I will."

He found an empty turtle shell and hung it up on a low branch. Then he beat on the shell with his horns.

"This is my elephant-scaring drum. I shall beat it, clatter, clatter," he said. "Elephant will run away. Oh, good, good, good."

Stamp, stamp, stamp. Along came Elephant.

Goat tossed his head and ran at the shell, clatter, clatter, beating it with his horns.

"Oh, what a clatter I'm making," he bleated. "Oh, what a terrible, elephant-scaring, horrible clatter."

Elephant said, "*What* a nasty little noise!"

He took the shell in his long trunk, lifted it high up into the air, and banged it down on Goat's hairy head. Then he went on his way, stamping.

Mouse said nothing. But she thought, "Poor old Goat looks sad, standing there with a shell on his head." Then she sat down on the grass and listened while Snake told his plan.

"I shall make myself into a rope," said Snake. "Yes, yes, yes, that's what I'll do." He looped his body around a tree trunk. "Now I'm an elephant-catching rope. Yes, yes, yes, that's what I am. I shall hold old Elephant tight by the leg, and I shan't let him go. No, I shan't let him go, till he promises not to stamp any more."

Stamp, stamp, stamp. Along came Elephant.

Snake hid in the long grass. Elephant stopped beside a tree, propped up his two white tusks on a branch, and settled himself for a nice little sleep.

Snake came gliding out of the grass. He looped his long body around the tree trunk and around old Elephant's leg as well. His teeth met his tail at the end of the loop, and he bit on his tail tip, holding fast.

"I have looped old Elephant's leg to the tree trunk. Now I must hold on tight," he thought.

Elephant woke, and tried to move. But with only three legs he was helpless.

"Why are you holding my leg?" he shouted.

Snake kept quiet. He could not speak. If he opened his mouth the loop would break.

Elephant put his trunk to the ground and filled it with tickling, yellow dust. Then he snorted, and blew the dust at Snake.

Snake wriggled. He wanted to sneeze.

Elephant put his trunk to the ground and sniffed up more of the tickling dust. "Poof!" he said, and he blew it at Snake.

Snake held his breath and wriggled and squirmed, trying his hardest not to sneeze. But the dust was too tickly. "Ah ah ah!" He closed his eyes and opened his mouth. "Ah ah tishoo!" The loop was broken.

Elephant said, "*What* a nasty little cold!"
And he went on his way, stamping.

Mouse said nothing. But she thought, "Snake looks sad, lying there sneezing his head off." Then she sat on the grass and made her own plan.

Stamp, stamp, stamp. Along came Elephant. Mouse peeped out of her hole and watched him. He lay on his side, stretched out his legs, and settled himself for a nice long sleep.

Mouse breathed deeply, and stiffened her whiskers. She waited till Elephant closed his eyes. Then she crept through the grass like a little grey shadow, her bright brown eyes watching Elephant's trunk. She made her way slowly around his great feet, and tiptoed past his shining tusks. She trotted along by his leathery trunk until she was close to its tender pink tip. Then suddenly, skip! She darted backwards, and sat in the end of Elephant's trunk.

Elephant opened his eyes, and said: "Can't I have *any* peace in this jungle? First it's a silly clattering goat, then it's a sillier, sneezing snake, and now it's a mouse, the smallest of them all, and quite the silliest. That's what *I* think."

He looked down his long grey trunk and said, "Oh yes, I know you are there, little mouse, because I can see your nose and whiskers. Out you get! Do you hear, little mouse?"

"Eek," said Mouse, "I won't get out, unless you promise not to stamp."

"Then I'll shake you out," Elephant shouted, and he swung his trunk from side to side.

"Thank you," squeaked Mouse, "I'm having a ride. It's almost like flying. Thank you, Elephant."

Elephant shouted, "I'll drown you out." He stamped to the river and waded in, dipping the end of his trunk in the water.

"Thank you," squeaked Mouse, "I'm having a swim. It's almost like diving. Thank you, Elephant."

Elephant stood on the bank, thinking. He could not pull down the leaves for his dinner. He could not give himself a bath. He could not live, with a mouse in his trunk.

"Please, little mouse, get out of my trunk. Please," he said.

40

"Will you promise not to stamp?" asked Mouse.

"No," said Elephant.

"Then this is what I shall do," said Mouse, and she tickled his trunk with her tail.

"Now will you promise not to stamp?"

"No," said Elephant.

"Then this is what I shall do," said Mouse and she nipped his trunk with her sharp little teeth.

"Yes," squealed Elephant. "Yes, yes, yes."

Mouse ran back to her hole and waited.

Step, step, step. Along came Elephant, walking gently on great grey feet. He saw the tiny shiny creatures, and waited until they scuttled away. He saw the little creeping creatures, and stepped very carefully over their tails.

"Elephant doesn't stamp any more. *Someone* has stopped him," the creatures said. "Someone big and brave and clever."

Goat said: "I think Mouse did it."

And Snake said: "Oh yes, that is right. Mouse did it."

And not far away, at the foot of a tree, a small, contented, tired little Mouse sat on the grass and smiled to herself.

Anita Hewett

Elmer, the Patchwork Elephant

In the herd of happy elephants there were large elephants and there were small elephants. There were old elephants and young elephants, elephants with long legs and elephants with short legs, elephants with flappy ears and elephants like this, that, and the other. But they were all the same colour, or very nearly so. All, that is, except Elmer.

Elmer was different. Elmer was patchwork. Elmer was yellow and orange and red and pink and purple and blue and green and black and white but NOT elephant colour.

It was Elmer who made the elephants laugh. Sometimes he joked with the other elephants, and sometimes they joked about him. But if there was even a little smile it was usually Elmer who started it.

One night Elmer couldn't sleep for thinking, and the think he was thinking was that he was tired of being different. He wanted to be like the other elephants. Who ever heard of a patchwork elephant? No wonder everyone laughed at him.

In the morning Elmer slipped quietly away so that none of the other elephants knew he had gone.

He walked and he walked and as he walked he met other animals. There was a lion who said, "Good morning, Elmer," and a tiger who said, "Good morning, Elmer."

A hippo, a giraffe, a zebra, a crocodile, and a tortoise all said, "Good morning, Elmer," too.

And each time Elmer smiled and said, "Good morning."

Midway through the morning a little bird flew by and said, "Where are you going so early, Elmer?"

"Somewhere," said Elmer. I want to be the same colour as the other elephants and I think I know how I can be. You can come along and help if you will."

Elmer walked and the bird rode. At last they stopped.

"This is what I've been looking for," Elmer said with a smile. There in front of him was a large bush covered with berries. The berries were elephant colour, not Elmer colour, but ordinary elephant colour.

Elmer shook the bush very hard with his trunk and berries fell and covered the ground. Slowly, Elmer lay down, then rolled over and over on the berries. They squashed, of course, and the colour started to cover Elmer.

Every now and then he asked the bird if all the old bright colours were gone. When the little bird would reply, "There's a patch of yellow on top of your head," or "there's some green under your chin," Elmer would rub some berries on his head or under his chin until at last the yellow and orange and red and pink and purple and blue and green and

black and white had all been covered — and Elmer looked like any other elephant.

Elmer said, "Thank you," to the bird, and walked back through the jungle to the herd of happy elephants.

As he walked, Elmer passed the other animals again. "Good morning, elephant," said the crocodile. "Good morning, elephant," said the tortoise. "Good morning, elephant," said the zebra, the hippo, the giraffe, the tiger and the lion. Elmer smiled and said, "Good morning," pleased that none of the other animals recognized him.

When he reached the elephant herd Elmer joined them, unnoticed. At first Elmer stayed at the edge of the herd, afraid that his disguise would be seen through. Gradually he became bolder and worked his way right into the middle of the herd. Still, none of the elephants recognized him. Elmer was delighted. After a while Elmer began to feel that something was wrong, but he didn't know what it was. The jungle looked the same. The sky looked the same with the same shining sun — true there was a big black cloud, but that was not unusual — so the only thing left was the herd of elephants. Elmer looked at them.

The elephants were standing absolutely still, and silent. Elmer realized what it was that seemed wrong; he'd never seen the elephants like this before, so lifeless. Elmer grinned to himself. And the more he looked at the serious, silent, standing-still elephants the more he wanted to laugh. Finally, Elmer could bear it no longer, and lifting his trunk

up high, and as loud as he could, he shouted: **BOOO!**

The poor elephants jumped and shook and fell down and rolled over in surprise. "Oh, my gosh and golly," they said, and looked at Elmer who was helpless with laughter. "Elmer!" they said. "It must be Elmer." Now the other elephants laughed, too. They laughed and laughed as they had never laughed before.

In the middle of the laughing the big black cloud burst and rain poured down and as it rained on Elmer his new colour washed off. Gradually the patchwork started to show again. The elephants laughed. The rain rained. Elmer became brighter and brighter until he was back to normal.

"Oh Elmer," gasped an elephant, "you have made some wonderful jokes before, but this has been our biggest laugh of all. It didn't take you long to show your true colours."

"We must celebrate this day every year," said another elephant. "It will be Elmer's day. All elephants must decorate themselves with bright-coloured patterns, and Elmer must decorate himself with ordinary elephant colour."

And this is exactly what elephants do. One day a year they have a carnival. They all decorate themselves with bright-coloured patterns, and on that day, if you happen to see an elephant who is ordinary elephant colour, you will know it must be Elmer.

David McKee

The Story of Babar

In the Great Forest a little elephant was born. His name was Babar. His mother loved him dearly, and used to rock him to sleep with her trunk, singing to him softly the while.

Babar grew fast. Soon he was playing with the other baby elephants. He was one of the nicest of them.

One day Babar was having a lovely ride on his mother's back, when a cruel hunter, hiding behind a bush, shot at them. He killed Babar's mother. The monkey hid himself, the birds flew away, and Babar burst into tears. The hunter ran up to catch poor Babar.

Babar was very frightened and ran away from the hunter. After some days, tired and footsore, he came to a town. He was amazed, for it was the first time he had ever seen so many houses. What strange things he saw! Beautiful avenues! Motorcars and motorbuses! But what interested Babar most of all was two gentlemen he met in the street. He thought to himself: "What lovely clothes they have got! I wish I could have some too! But how can I get them?"

Luckily, he was seen by a very rich old lady who understood little elephants, and knew at once that he was longing for a smart suit. She loved making others happy, so she gave him her purse.

"Thank you, Madam," said Babar.

Without wasting a moment Babar went into a big shop. He got into the lift. It was such fun going up and down in this jolly little box, that he went ten times to the very top and ten times down again to the bottom. He was going up once more when the lift-boy said to him: "Sir, this is not a toy. You must get out now and buy what you want. Look, here is the shop-walker." Then he bought a shirt, collar and tie, a suit of a delightful green colour, next a lovely bowler hat, and finally shoes and spats. Babar was so pleased with his purchases, and satisfied with his appearance that he paid a visit to the photographer. And here is his photograph.

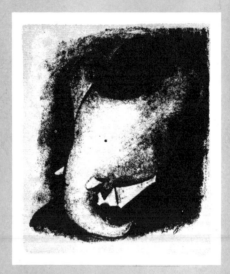

Babar went to dinner with his friend the old lady. She, too, thought he looked very smart in his new suit. After dinner, he was so tired, that he went early to sleep.

Babar made his home in the old lady's house. Every morning they did their exercises together, and then Babar had his bath. Every day he drove out in the car that the old lady had bought him. She gave him everything that he wanted.

A learned professor gave him lessons. Babar was attentive, and always gave the right answer. He was a most promising pupil.

In the evenings, after dinner, he told the old lady's friends all about his life in the Great Forest. And yet Babar was not altogether happy: he could no longer play about in the Great Forest with his little cousins and his friends the monkeys. He often gazed out of the window, dreaming of his childhood, and when he thought of his dear mother he used to cry.

Two years passed by. One day he was out for a walk, when he met two little elephants with no clothes on. "Why, here are Arthur and Celeste, my two little cousins!" he cried in amazement to the old lady.

Babar hugged Arthur and Celeste and took them to buy some lovely clothes. Next he took them to a tea-shop, where they had some delicious cakes. Meanwhile in the Great Forest all the elephants were searching for Arthur and Celeste and their mothers grew more and more anxious. Luckily an old bird flying over the town had spied them, and hurried back to tell the elephants. The mothers went to the town to fetch Arthur and Celeste. They were glad when they found them, but scolded them all the same for having run away.

Babar made up his mind to return to the Great Forest with Arthur and Celeste and their mothers. The old lady helped him to pack.

When everything was ready for the journey Babar kissed his old friend good-bye. If he had not been so sorry to leave her he would have been delighted to go home. He promised to come back to her, and never to forget her.

Off they went! There was no room for the mother elephants in the car. So they ran behind, lifting their trunks so as not to breathe in the dust. The old lady was left alone, sadly thinking: "When shall I see my little Babar again?"

Alas! That very day the King of the elephants had eaten a bad mushroom. It had poisoned him. He had been very ill, and then had died. It was a terrible misfortune. After his funeral the oldest elephants met together to choose a new King.

Just at that moment they heard a noise and turned round. What a wonderful sight they saw! It was Babar arriving in his car, with all the elephants running and shouting: "Here they are! Here they are! They have come back! Hullo, Babar! Hullo, Arthur! Hullo, Celeste! What lovely clothes! What a beautiful car!"

Then Cornelius, the oldest elephant of all, said, in his

quavering voice: "My dear friends, we must have a new King. Why not choose Babar? He has come back from the town, where he has lived among men and learnt much. Let us offer him the crown." All the elephants thought that Cornelius had spoken wisely, and they listened eagerly to hear what Babar would say.

"I thank you all," said Babar; "but before accepting the crown I must tell you that on our journey in the car Celeste and I got engaged to be married. If I become your King, she will be your Queen."

Long live Queen Celeste! Long live King Babar!!

The elephants shouted with one voice. And that was how Babar became King.

"Cornelius," said Babar, "you have such good ideas that I shall make you a general, and when I get my crown I will give you my hat. In a week's time I am going to marry Celeste. We will give a grand party to celebrate our marriage and our coronation." And Babar asked the birds to take invitations to all the animals, and he told the dromedary to go to the town to buy him some fine wedding clothes.

The guests began to arrive. The dromedary brought the clothes just in time for the ceremony. After the wedding and the coronation everyone danced merrily.

The Party was over. Night fell, and the stars came out. The hearts of King Babar and Queen Celeste were filled with happy dreams.

Then all the world slept. The guests had gone home, very pleased and very tired after dancing so much. For many a long day they will remember that wonderful ball.

Then King Babar and Queen Celeste set out on their honeymoon, in a glorious yellow balloon, to meet with new adventures.

Jean de Brunhoff

The Story of Dumbo

It was August and the circus was in town. All the children were there eating ice-creams and enjoying the clowns and the tightrope walkers and the lions, but most of all, they were enjoying Dumbo.

Now, Dumbo was a little elephant. But he was no ordinary little elephant. He had enormous ears, so enormous that he could fly. He was, in fact, the only flying elephant in the whole world.

Round and round the ring he would fly. On Dumbo's
trunk would sit Timothy Mouse, who was his best friend,
holding a flag with a big D on it, which stood for Dumbo.

But Dumbo was not really very happy. People kept
laughing at him because his ears were so big. This made him
very sad because all he really wanted was to be an ordinary
elephant like his mother and father.

One day he was sitting in the big top, feeling very sorry for himself, when up popped Timothy.

"You don't look very happy," said Timothy.

"I'm tired of people laughing at me."

"Never mind," said Timothy, "I don't like the circus much either, let's fly away. They'll never catch us."

Dumbo's face lit up. He thought this was a splendid idea. "Why not," he said. "Let's go this very night."

Timothy led Dumbo out of the big top by his trunk, and in no time at all they were flying away into the night. The moon was out as they flew high above the roof tops. Timothy sat on Dumbo's trunk, just as he did in their circus act, but this time it was different. This time they were really free. They flew on and on, further and further from the circus, until eventually Dumbo's ears were very tired.

"I can't go on any longer," he said. "Let's have a rest somewhere."

"There's a tree over there," shouted Timothy. "Let's sleep in the branches. There they slept for the rest of the night. When they awoke Dumbo decided it was time to play.

"Look at those boys and girls over there," he said. "Let's go over and join them." Timothy agreed and off they flew to join the children, or rather their kites.

The kites were all different colours, red and yellow and blue. "I wish I was a nice bright colour," said Dumbo. "But then again, I can fly without a piece of string."

The boys and girls shouted, "Come on down, we won't hurt you." So Dumbo flapped his ears gently and landed.

"Isn't he sweet," said one of the girls.

Dumbo smiled happily, thinking he had found some new friends. But he hadn't noticed that one of the boys was tying a piece of rope round his neck.

"Let's fly him," shouted the boy. "With ears like that he should fly just like a kite."

"Oh, please don't," pleaded Dumbo. "It's not fair, I don't want to be flown like a kite."

But the boys were very unkind and they ran along across the field pulling Dumbo behind them. Sure enough, after a while, Dumbo started to drift into the air.

"Let me down," he wailed, "please let me down. I'm frightened."

"No fear," shouted one of the boys. "We've got the best kite in the world now, and we're not going to let you go!"

"But I'm NOT a kite," sobbed Dumbo, "I'm an elephant!"

Suddenly, just as Dumbo was giving up hope, he heard a little voice from just below him.

"Never mind, Dumbo, I'll get you out of this." It was Timothy, who was clinging to the rope just below Dumbo's neck.

"I'll chew my way through the rope in no time," said Timothy bravely. He chewed and chewed until SNAP! the rope broke and Dumbo was free again.

"Let's get away from here," he said.

So off they flew over the fields and meadows with Timothy sitting triumphantly on Dumbo's trunk.

Without Timothy, Dumbo felt he would be quite defeated by all the cruel people in the world. But while he flew high above danger, with Timothy cheering him on, he was completely happy. "Where to?" shouted Dumbo, as though he were a taxi driver.

"To the Land of Happiness!" replied Timothy. "Don't stop until you get there."

The two friends flew all that day. At last, Dumbo became slower and more tired and they found themselves drifting only just above the ground.

"I must drop down soon," said Dumbo with a weary sigh.

"All right," said Timothy. "This looks like a comfortable place to land." It was getting dark, but Dumbo gently came to land in a hayfield.

"Oh-h! Oh-h-h!" said Dumbo to his friend. "Have you ever smelt such fresh, sweet hay?"

"Yes, Yes," said Timothy impatiently. He was much too tired to talk about it. Early next morning, Dumbo was

awakened suddenly by a sharp prod in his side, and the first thing he saw was a three-pronged fork only inches from his face. It was held by a bad-tempered looking farmer.

"Up you get, whoever you are" ordered the farmer unpleasantly. "Anyone found sleeping in my fields goes straight to work for me." Dumbo was so dismayed that he turned to Timothy to see what he was thinking. "I can't have mice in my field," snapped the farmer. "I'll soon have you chased out of here." And before Dumbo knew what was happening, the farmer poked his fork towards Timothy, who shot out of Dumbo's hat and ran for his life, leaving Dumbo quaking.

The farmer harnessed poor Dumbo to a haywagon, and made him pull heavy loads all day. At nightfall, he chained him with the other animals to a stall in the barn.

During the night, there was a scratching sound that made Dumbo sit up and listen. All at once, he heard the scurry of Timothy's little feet, and the loyal little mouse appeared. As soon as he saw him, Dumbo began to weep. "Oh, what are we going to do now, Timothy?" he asked in despair.

"Don't worry. I always have rescued you, haven't I? I'll think of something, and then we'll go on and find the Land of Happiness."

"I don't want to find it," said Dumbo. "I want to go back to my mother."

Timothy thought sadly that that might be the best thing to do. After all, they did not even know where the Land of Happiness was. But first he must get Dumbo free from his chain.

Hiding carefully from the farmer, Timothy looked around the field for someone who could help. There were two crows flying around who had been watching Dumbo with pity.

"Poor little fellow," they said to each other. "If only he could fly like us, he could just up and disappear."

"He *can* fly!" shouted Timothy, when he heard what they were saying. "He *can* fly! But we've got to get him out of those chains."

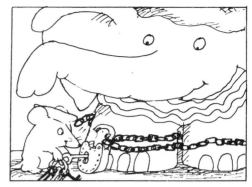

"Leave it to us," said the crows, delighted at some excitement in store. Quickly they decided on a plan.

They flew down on the farmer's head when he appeared, and flustered him until his keys fell out of his pocket. Timothy grabbed the keys, sped towards Dumbo and tried every one until he found the key for the chain. Then Dumbo was suddenly free!

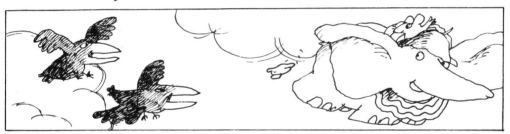

He only just remembered to wait for Timothy to catch on to his trunk before he zoomed into the air, leaving the cruel farmer stunned and angry in his field. The two crows caught up with him and called out, "Where are you heading for?"

"For home," Dumbo shouted, "and my mother." And with that he disappeared away into the blue sky in the direction of the circus.

Dumbo's mother had been sorrowing for her son since he had left the circus, and the ringmaster had decided that if ever the baby elephant returned, he would give him a star part in the circus. He could not persuade Mrs Jumbo to work happily until Dumbo's safe return.

They did not know that Dumbo was only minutes away from them at that moment. They couldn't believe their eyes when he at last reached the circus. Dumbo and his mother both wept from joy. Dumbo did not care whether he was laughed at or not, he just wanted to be beside his mother for always.

The ringmaster was as good as his word. Mrs Jumbo would be happy at her work again, and that was good enough for him. He gave Dumbo the star part in the performance that very night, and Dumbo gave a show that even the ringmaster was very proud of.

Timothy Mouse was installed as Dumbo's manager, and made sure that he had everything a star should have. Dumbo was given a caravan to himself, furnished in true star fashion, and his mother lived with him in comfort, proud to have such a famous son.

Timothy Mouse was glad to be back at his work. He had enjoyed his adventures with Dumbo the Flying Elephant, but he had enough to remember and think about for the rest of his life.

Walt Disney

The Blind Men and the Elephant

It was six men of Indostan
To learning much inclined,
Who went to see the Elephant
(Though all of them were blind),
That each by observation
Might satisfy his mind.

The *First* approached the Elephant,
And happening to fall
Against his broad and sturdy side,
At once began to bawl:
"God bless me! — but the Elephant
Is very like a wall!"

The *Second* feeling of the tusk,
Cried "Ho! — what have we here
So very round and smooth and sharp?
To me 'tis mighty clear
This wonder of an Elephant
Is very like a spear!"

The *Third* approached the animal,
And happening to take
The squirming trunk within his hands,
Thus boldly up and spake:
"I see," quoth he, "the Elephant
Is very like a snake!"

The *Fourth* reached out his eager hand,
And felt about the knee.
"What most this mighty beast is like
Is mighty plain." quoth he;
"'Tis clear enough the Elephant
Is very like a tree!"

The *Fifth* who chanced to touch the ear,
Said: "E'en the blindest man
Can tell what this resembles most;
Deny the fact who can,
This marvel of an Elephant
Is very like a fan!"

The *Sixth* no sooner had begun
About the beast to grope,
Than, seizing on the swinging tail
That fell within his scope,
"I see," quoth he, "the Elephant
Is very like a rope!"

And so these men of Indostan
Disputed loud and long,
Each in his own opinion
Exceeding stiff and strong,
Though each was partly in the right,
And *all* were in the wrong!

                                    J. G. Saxe